Written and illustrated by
Colin West

Reprinted 2007, 2008
First paperback edition 2006
First published 2005 by
A & C Black Publishers Ltd
38 Soho Square, London, W1D 3HB

www.acblack.com

ISBN 978-0-7136-7327-2

A CIP catalogue for this book is available from the British Library.

This book is produced using paper made from wood
grown in managed, sustainable forests. It is natural, renewable
and recyclable. The logging and manufacturing processes conform
to the environmental regulations of the country of origin.

Printed and bound in China by South China Printing Co., Ltd.

Chapter One

Toby wanted to be a sailor, but he didn't know much about the sea, and all he had for a boat was an old tin bathtub.

One day, Toby was feeling very
adventurous. He paddled his tub an
extra long way out from his home
in Puddledock Beach.

He spent some time drifting around...

... trying to think up a name for his
trusty tub...

Soon Toby fell fast asleep…

It was about tea-time when Toby finally woke up. He was disappointed he hadn't come up with a good name for his tub.

Then he looked about and, to his horror, he realised he couldn't see the shore!

The sky was getting darker and the sea was getting rougher. Then there was a clap of thunder and a flash of lightning.

Toby's tiny tub was tossed up and down
by the huge waves.

Chapter Two

The storm raged all night long, but somehow Toby's tub survived.
Slowly, the clouds disappeared and the sea became calm again.

When Toby looked around, he saw he was in a very strange place...

There were tall icebergs towering over him, and in the distance was a big island. Close by it were two smaller islands.

As Toby paddled towards the small islands, he could see they weren't made of ice or rock or sand.

Toby prodded one of them with his oar.
He had the shock of his life when
suddenly it moved!

"OUCH!" bellowed a mighty voice.
And, looming above him, Toby saw the
face of a massive Sea Giant. He realised
he'd just prodded the Giant's kneecap.
Toby was frightened.

But there was something about the Sea Giant that didn't make him look fierce and mean. He looked miserable.

Toby realised there was no need to be scared. This was a harmless giant. "What's the matter?" asked Toby. "It's a long story…" replied the Sea Giant, whose name was Blubber.

Chapter Three

It seemed that almost two hundred years ago, King Krug, the King of all Sea Giants, had placed Blubber in charge of the island of Dumbfoundland.

The map shows:
The Echoless Icebergs, Big Hush Harbour, The Quiet Caves, The Sleeping Burrows, The Voiceless Rocks, Dumbfoundland

Now, Dumbfoundland was a special sort
of place. It was home to lots of very odd
creatures, but they were all fast asleep
in secret caves and burrows. And it
needed a magic sound to wake them up.

Unfortunately, no one knew what the magic sound was. Blubber was desperate for some friends. So, for two hundred years, he'd been trying all the noises he could think of to wake up the animals.

Blubber had tried…

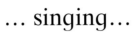… singing…

… and howling…

… and screaming…

… and growling.

And he'd tried yelling and barking and roaring and squawking…

… and also wailing and mooing and
hissing and booing…

And not forgetting…

… coughing…

… and sneezing…

… and sniffing…

… and wheezing.

But Dumbfoundland had remained as sleepy as ever. So Blubber had tried making up new noises.

He'd thurped and thoogled, and woppled and googled. But *still* it was no use.

Blubber was really lonely.

Finally, he'd sobbed and sighed and moaned and cried from being all alone for two hundred years.

Chapter Four

Toby could see just how sad the Sea
Giant was. He thought the best thing to
do was to cheer him up.
So Toby told Blubber the funniest joke
he knew.

At first the Sea Giant began to chuckle
to himself. Then his laughter grew louder
and his huge body started shaking.
He wriggled his toes and he
thumped his knees.

And he laughed so much that he started
to hiccup.

They were the loudest hiccups Toby had ever heard.

And as the hiccups echoed all around,
Toby heard a flapping noise and a
splashing sound. And then it happened...

A strange bird flew overhead…

… and a funny fish
leapt out of the water.

Chapter Five

Toby suddenly realised that the sound of hiccups was the magic sound that would wake up all the strange animals.

So Toby told more and more jokes to Blubber as fast as he could.

What's yellow and dangerous?
Shark-infested custard!

How does a lolly get to school?
On an ice-cycle!

Which fish sleeps a lot?
A kipper!

What do scientists eat?
Microchips!

What's hairy and wears sunglasses?
A coconut on holiday!

What's green and points north?
A magnetic cucumber!

What's the fastest vegetable?
A runner bean!

What do ghosts eat for supper?
Ghoulash!

Blubber couldn't stop laughing. And the more he laughed, the more he hiccupped.

And the more he hiccupped, the more the strange birds flapped and the more the funny fish splashed.

Then some *really* odd creatures started
appearing from the hidden caves
and the secret burrows.

There were all sorts, such as…

… the Green
Thingy…

… the Oink…

… the Willet…

… the Rippersaurus…

… the Slopp…

… the Great Thump…

… and the Wasseltrope.

Blubber was the happiest Sea Giant
in the world, as he played with all his
new-found friends.

Toby could have stayed all day, but he knew he should be getting home. So he waved goodbye and paddled away in his old tin tub.

Chapter Six

As the sound of hiccups faded into the distance, Toby realised he still hadn't thought up a name for his tub. So that's what he tried to do.

Suddenly Toby had something else to
think about. He noticed that a thick fog
was falling.

Soon Toby couldn't see a thing, but he
kept on paddling.

After a long, long time, Toby could just
make out a dim light in the distance.

As he came closer, he could see it was
coming from a lighthouse.

He was back home at Puddledock Beach!

And as he recalled his adventure, Toby
suddenly knew what to call his old tin tub
– "The Hiccup", of course!